Mystery

ARTHUR GEISERT

Houghton Mifflin Company Boston 2003

Walter Lorraine Books

For Doris, Bonnie, and Darlene

Walter Lorraine (wr) Books

Copyright © 2003 by Arthur Geisert

www.houghtonmifflinbooks.com

Library of Congress Cataloging-in-Publication Data

Geisert, Arthur.
    Mystery / Arthur Geisert.
        p. cm.
    Summary: During a visit to the art museum, a little piglet and her
grandfather investigate the disappearance of several paintings. Clues in
the illustrations give readers a chance to solve the mystery along with
the heroine.
    ISBN 0-618-27293-3
    [1. Art museums—Fiction. 2. Museums—Fiction. 3. Pigs—Fiction. 4.
Grandfathers—Fiction. 5. Mystery and detective stories. 6. Picture
puzzles.] I. Title.
    PZ7.G2724Ir 2003
    [E]—dc21

                                                            2003000179

Printed in the United States of America
WOZ 10 9 8 7 6 5 4 3 2 1

Mystery

I packed the lunch—sandwiches with extra mayonnaise, apples, oranges, and twenty-four cookies. Everything my grandpa liked. He was taking me to the museum for copying day.

Copying day was every Tuesday morning.

The museum was closed, but artists could come
and draw and paint the collection.

Grandpa went off to the large painting gallery.

"Don't lose the lunch," he told me.

I liked to draw.

Grandpa told me to join him after I finished my raccoon drawing.

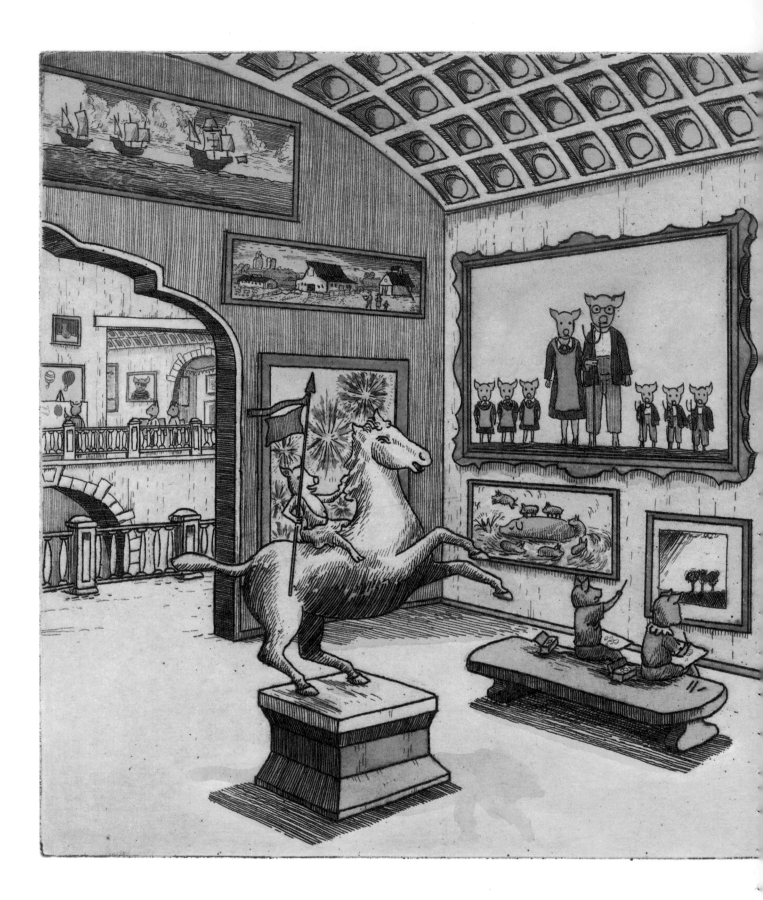

Grandpa said he wanted to copy the haystack painting.

When I joined him, he was busy copying. I looked for something
to draw. Then I noticed something funny.

I got Grandpa. He saw it too. He went to get the museum guards.
They were very upset. Pieces of the paintings were missing
and had been replaced with not so very good patches.

I noticed tracks and scratches. The guards said
some of the scratches looked like ladder marks.

We found the ladder. The same tracks were all around it.
There was also some long, coarse hair stuck in the ladder
and an apple core nearby.

We took the ladder back to the gallery.
We found more paintings that had been damaged.

We found more tracks, scratches, and hair, too.

After I told them they looked like raccoon tracks, they suspected the raccoon who lived in the apple tree just outside the museum. They went to get him.

Grandpa told me to come along with them.

They searched the tree, but they didn't find the raccoon.
I found an apple core. And I saw some curious little holes.

Suddenly I had a thought. I yelled, "Stop! The raccoon didn't do it! Let me show you my drawings. I think you'll see what I see."

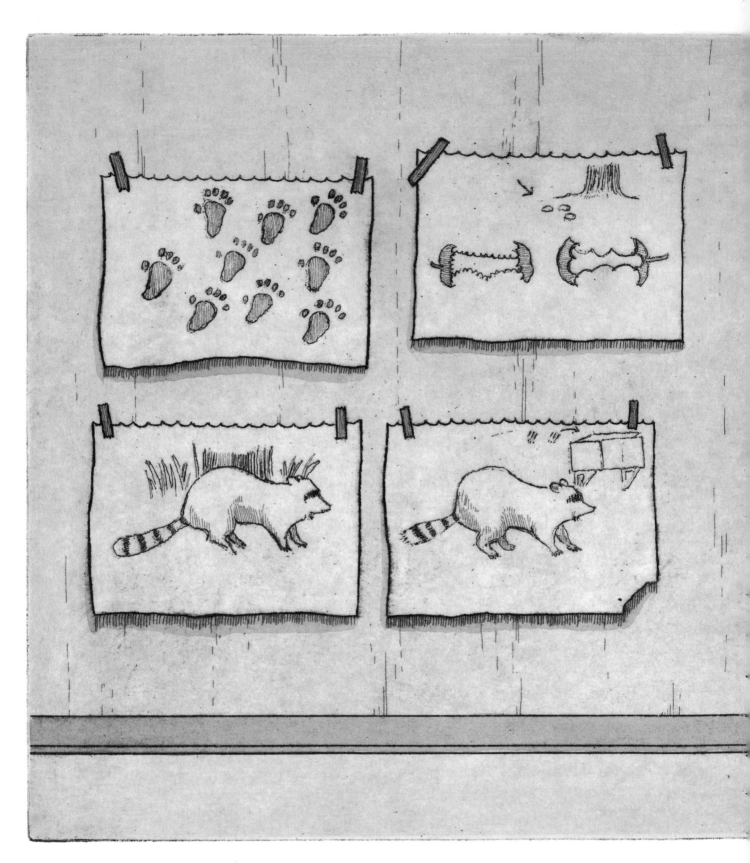

I taped my drawings to a wall.
But they still didn't see what I wanted them to.

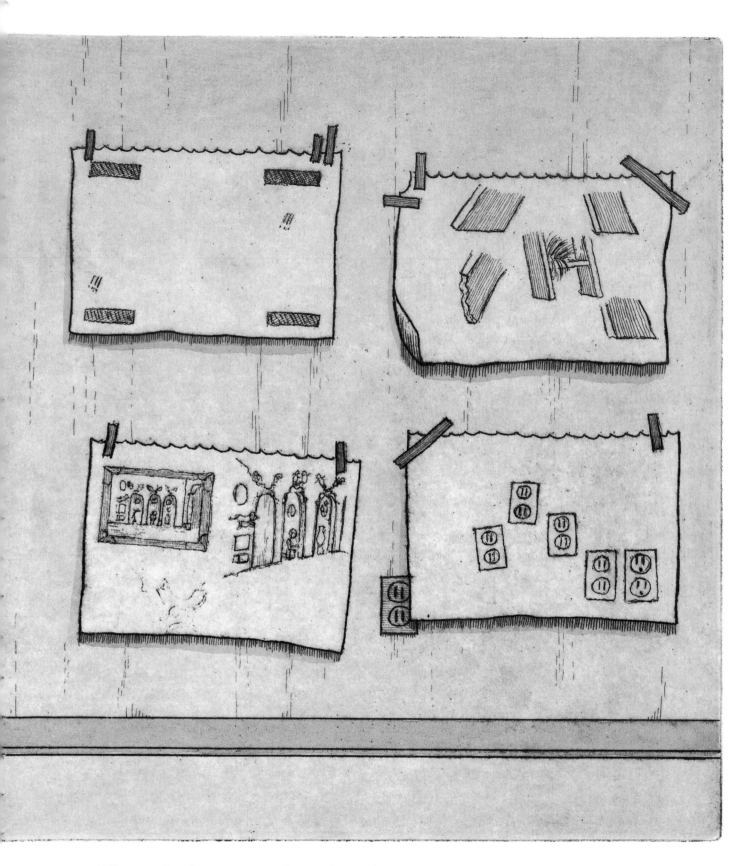

They asked me to explain. So I did . . .

"All the tracks have the big toe on the same side. The apple core in
the closet has little gnaw marks. The apple core by the tree has big
gnaw marks. A piece of the stuffed raccoon's tail is missing.
The supposed ladder scratches look like this. The ladder has one

broken leg and wouldn't make four marks the same. The alcove, walled up since the earthquake, has a funny electrical outlet— different from all the others. I've seen little scratches everywhere we've gone. I think whoever did this is behind the outlet."

The guards checked the outlet. It was fake.
What they saw surprised them.

They took sledgehammers and broke a hole into the wall.

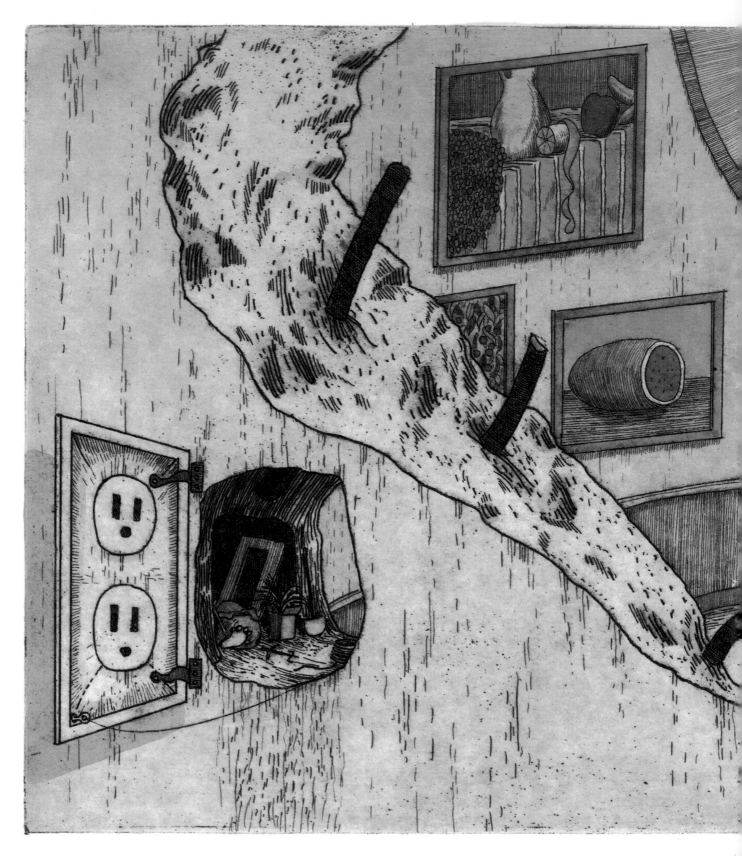

All of the evidence was in a little hollowed-out closet.
The fake foot, a box of hair, crossbows and ropes, sacks of
dirt, and a shovel—they were all there.

Behind the wall was a formal mouse dining area.
On the walls were original paintings of food. All
were stolen from the museum.

After looking at the evidence, we determined the mice took photographs and painted copies. They made a fake raccoon paw to make footprints. They cut off the tip of the stuffed raccoon's tail. They made a stencil from a foot of the ladder.

They planted hair as evidence. They gnawed an apple and left the
core. The mice used a crossbow to shoot ropes into the frames so they
could get what they wanted. Other mice planted evidence. They
hoped if anyone noticed the theft, the raccoon would be blamed.

The mystery was solved. The museum gave me a lifetime pass.
Lunch was right where I had left it. The guards were on alert in
case the mice tried to pull something. That day I knew what
I wanted to be when I grew up—a police artist and a detective.